HOT WHEELS

RACE TO THE RESCUE!

Story by Ron Burch and David Kidd

studio fun
INTERNATIONAL

T5-CVG-766

In Hot Wheels City, there is chaos everywhere! Nevard, the super-secret super clone of arch villain Draven, has taken over the Ultimate Garage and is using a dragon and a giant gorilla to guard it. Sophia, Quinn, Chase, and Elliot are racing across town to face the villain.

Who created Draven's super-secret clone, and what do his evil plans have to do with the Ultimate Garage? The racers will have to find out!

"Keep up, we gotta get to the Ultimate Garage fast," Chase says as his car speeds through the street.

"I've got a blast of fast and a garage to save!" Sophia responds.

As the friends race their way to the Ultimate Garage, a giant scorpion appears and rears its ugly head! Scuttling out from behind a skyscraper, this huge bug is going to sting.

"I thought we beat this thing before!" Chase yells.

"Then we can do it again!" Sophia says.

The four racers confront the scorpion, making it spin in circles by driving and weaving between its legs. When it's finally distracted, Sophia drives up the scorpion's tail and onto its head.

"Steady, Sophia. Here it comes!" Quinn calls out. The scorpion swings its stinger to throw Sophia off, but accidentally stings itself instead!

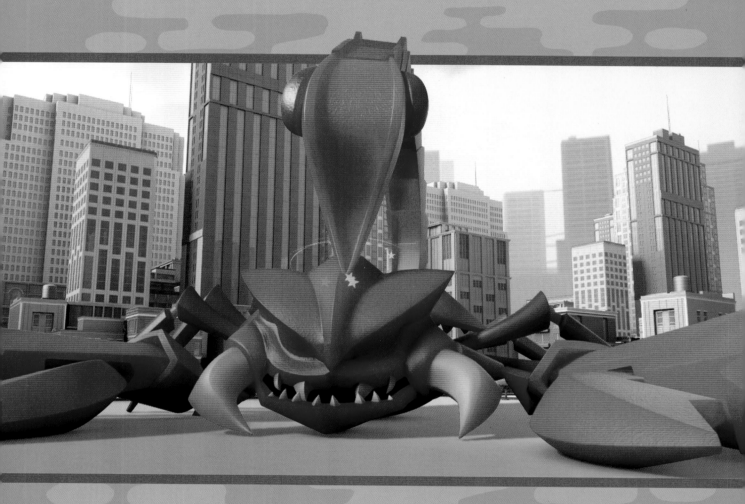

"That monster is going to have a monster headache when it wakes up," Elliot says.

"Yeah," Quinn says, "let's not be here for that."

The racers speed off to confront Nevard at the Ultimate Garage, but when they arrive, they see the giant gorilla and the dangerous dragon guarding it!

"Like what I've done with the place?" he calls out, standing between the two beasts.

"Why is it glowing?" Quinn asks. "Did you mess with my systems, Nevard?"

"Improved, more like it. You never understood the power of the Tetra-flame," he responds.

Just then, the dragon lets out a fire-breathing roar!

As the crew is trying its best to figure out what Nevard is up to, a report comes in that weird objects—like giant ice cream cones and robot dogs—are popping up all over the city. "We better check this out," Chase says. They jump back into their cars and drive off.

As Quinn, Sophia, Chase, and Elliot drive through the streets of Hot Wheels City, strange objects continue to appear in the middle of the street: a giant fire hydrant, weird trees, and even a flying ice cream truck!

"We need to get off this street," Sophia calls out to her friends.

They try to leave the street, but there are barricades everywhere and signs that lead them toward a detour.

They follow all the arrows, but it leads them straight to a dead end.

"Okay, who mapped this detour?" Chase asks.

Suddenly, a red Baja Bone Shaker Hot Wheels race car spins into the dead end, and the window rolls down to reveal a familiar face. "That would be me, I'm afraid," says Draven.

"Draven?!?" they all say in disbelief.

"You tricked us here!" Elliot calls out.

"Trapping you was the only way I could think of getting you to listen to me!" he responds.

Draven tells the crew that he is not the one responsible for what Nevard is doing, and he has no idea who made the super-secret evil clone. Quinn thinks there's only one way to get answers—they all need to team up and confront Nevard together.

"But he's a bad guy!" Elliot says.

"Elliot, the enemy of your enemy is your friend. At least for now," Chase responds.

"Agreed," Draven says with a smile.

Sophia, Quinn, Chase, Elliot, and their new ally Draven race across the city to take Nevard by surprise. But when they get there, a huge surprise is waiting for them.

It's a giant flying shark! It can fly, and it looks like it can even swim through the streets without crashing.

"We're going to need bigger cars," Chase says.

"And maybe a boat," Quinn responds.

The giant flying shark attacks the crew! They all speed through the track loops, doing their best to avoid all those chomping teeth.

"We need to get back to dry land," Chase calls out.

"I thought this was dry land!" Elliot says.

As they do their best to avoid the sharp-toothed attacker, they decide that they need to split up. Quinn and Draven head off to try to figure out what is going on with the Ultimate Garage, and the rest of the crew distracts the shark.

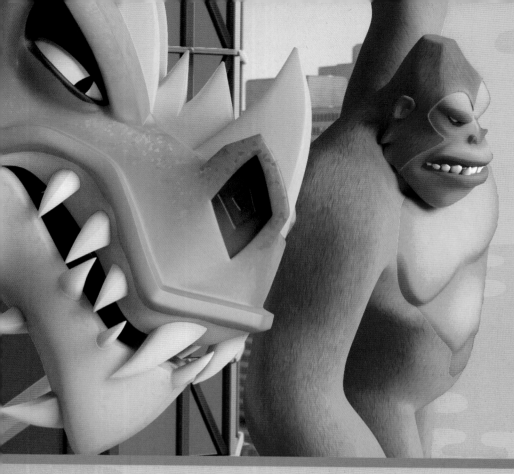

Quinn and Draven spin away, but they've got some monsters on their tail! The gorilla and dragon are back and determined to stop the two geniuses.

"I'll take the dragon; you take the gorilla. Then I'll meet you at the Impossible Jump," Draven says.

"Roger that," Quinn responds.

They split up to confront their foes with the new plan. Quinn versus the gorilla, and Draven versus the dragon. These monsters won't know what hit them!

The dragon lets out a stream of fire right onto Draven's car, but he's just fast enough to get away. He's leading the dragon to the Impossible Jump, and Quinn isn't far behind with the gorilla.

Finally, they both launch over the Impossible Jump, just barely missing each other. Then the gorilla and dragon collide in midair and come crashing to the ground! Confused, the dragon grabs the gorilla by the shoulders and flies away.

"Nicely done," Draven says.

But their triumph doesn't last long. They look up and see a glowing machine at the top of the Ultimate Garage.

"Is that a Tetra-amplifier?" Quinn asks in shock.

"That's why the Ultimate Garage is glowing! He's using the Tetra-flame to suck power from the entire city," Draven says.

Draven and Quinn don't know why Nevard needs so much power. But they do realize that they can use the shark to counteract all the heat the Tetra-flame is creating. With a plan in mind, they race back into the city to help the others defeat the shark.

Sophia, Chase, and Elliot are busy distracting the shark, but they are starting to get worried. If Quinn and Draven don't show up soon, they could run out of gas.

Suddenly, they hear the sound of an ice cream truck—and it's no regular sweet-mobile. Powered up with a freeze gun Quinn and Draven created, it shoots freeze bombs right through the jaws of the flying shark!

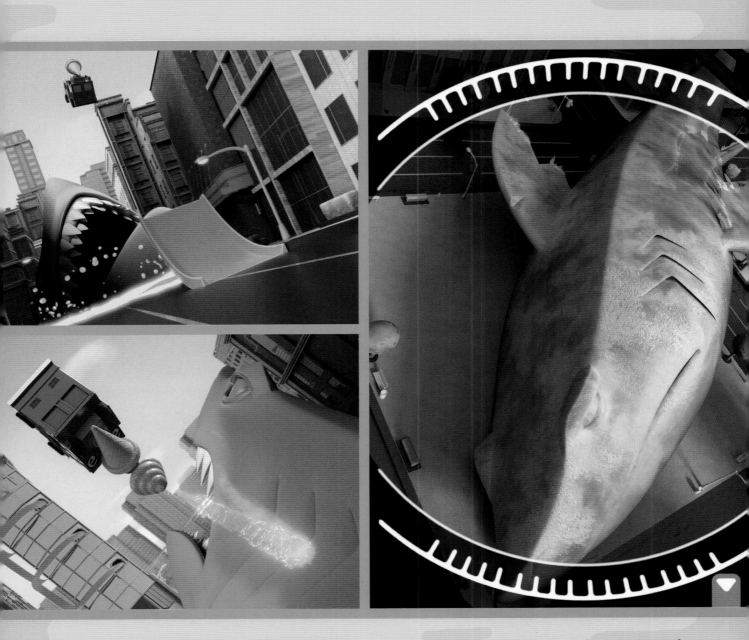

After two shots from the freeze gun, the shark crashes to the ground with a loud THUD. It has been neutralized!

"We caught the shark, but there's still another fish to fry. A bad one," Chase says, turning to face the Ultimate Garage. "We're coming for you, Nevard!"

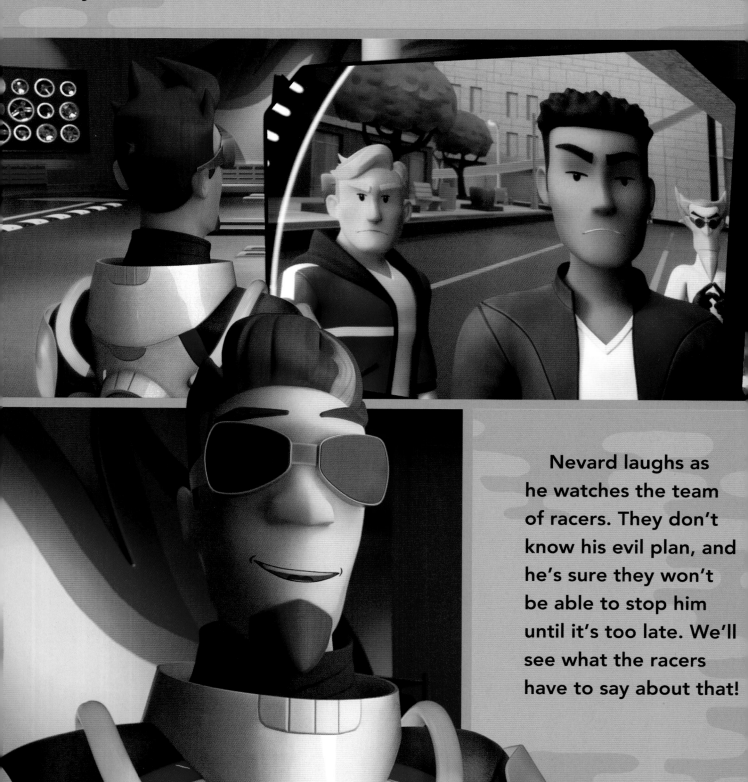

Nevard laughs as he watches the team of racers. They don't know his evil plan, and he's sure they won't be able to stop him until it's too late. We'll see what the racers have to say about that!

After the defeat of the super shark, more weird things happen all over Hot Wheels City. The buildings start glitching, and objects are popping into the street left and right. Even a huge teddy bear!

They go to the Mega Car Wash to fix up their cars and come up with a plan to defeat Nevard once and for all.

"He's causing a rift in the space-time continuum!" Draven yells.

"What?!?" everyone asks. "How do you know?"

"The glitches aren't just things from Hot Wheels City," Quinn responds. "They're things from who knows where . . . or when."

Draven points to the screen in front of him. "Take the giant shark. Species that large have been extinct for a hundred million years," he says.

"Nevard must be trying to bring something even bigger here to take over all of Hot Wheels City!" Chase says.

"We've got to stop him," Quinn says.

"Then we're going to need a blast of fast!" Sophia says.

"Challenged accepted!" Draven says. Everyone looks at him, confused. "I've always wanted to say that," he admits.

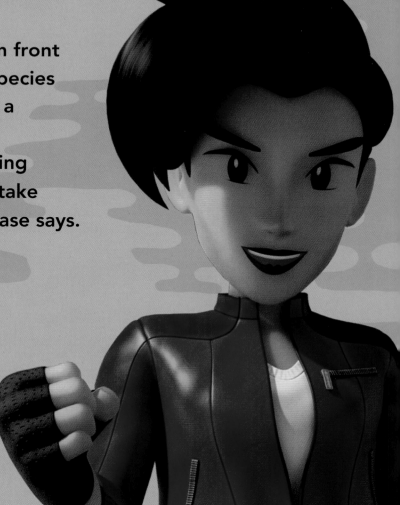

The racers make their way across the city to confront Nevard one last time. But it looks like all the giant beasts are back and ready for round two! Facing down the scorpion, gorilla, shark, and dragon all at once is not going to be easy.

"We've got to split them up, then pit them against each other!" Sophia says.

They all pick their opponents: Elliot versus the gorilla, Quinn versus the scorpion, Draven versus the dragon, and Chase and Sophia versus the super shark. They all speed off to complete their assignments. These monsters are fierce, but are they as fast as the racers?

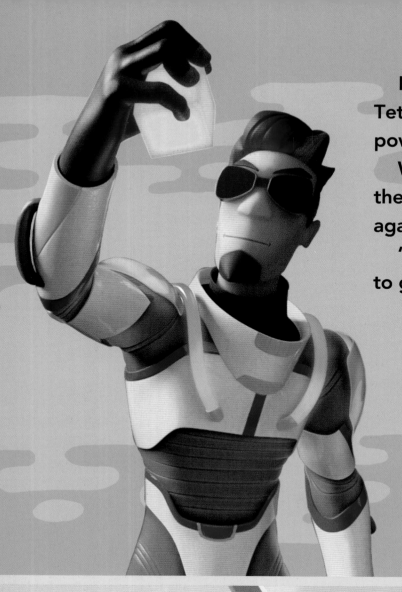

Meanwhile, Nevard is using the Tetra-amplifier to make a super powerful Tetra charger.

When the racers finally defeat all the monsters, they meet up and race against the clock to stop Nevard.

"Four monsters down, one evil clone to go," Quinn says.

But when they arrive at the Ultimate Garage, Nevard has finished making his Tetra charger and has plugged it into his race car.

"This is bad, really bad! But I've got an idea," Quinn says.

They all start racing Nevard through the streets of Hot Wheels City, and Sophia is right on his tail. Nevard speeds up, but he can't shake her. If anyone can catch him, she can.

"Go, Sophia!" Chase calls out.

Nevard is heading toward a giant portal in the middle of the sky! The racers have no idea where it leads, but there's no turning back now—they can't let Nevard get away.

They follow him straight through the portal!

Quinn, Sophia, Chase, Elliot, and Draven emerge from the portal, and they're somewhere . . . strange. "We did it!" Chase says. "Sophia, you did it! We saved Hot Wheels City!"

"But where are we?" Elliot asks.

"Or rather, when," Quinn says.

They look up at the super-awesome city around them, and that's when they realize what happened—Nevard has taken them through a portal to the future Hot Wheels City! They don't know what will happen next, but whatever comes their way, Sophia, Quinn, Chase, and Elliot will be sure to save Hot Wheels City every time.